Welcome to ALADDIN QUIX!

If you are looking for fast, fun-to-read stories with colorful characters, lots of kid-friendly humor, easy-to-follow action, entertaining story lines, and lively illustrations, then **ALADDIN QUIX** is for you!

But wait, there's more!

If you're also looking for stories with tables of contents; word lists; about-the-book questions; 64, 80, or 96 pages; short chapters; short paragraphs; and large fonts, then **ALADDIN QUIX** is *definitely* for you!

ALADDIN QUIX: The next step between ready to reads and longer, more challenging chapter books, for readers five to eight years old.

Read more ALADDIN QUIX books!

By Stephanie Calmenson

Our Principal Is a Frog!
Our Principal Is a Wolf!
Our Principal's in His Underwear!
Our Principal Breaks a Spell!

Fort Builders Inc.
By Dee Romito

Book 1: *The Birthday Castle*
Coming soon: *The Battle of the Blanket Forts*

A Miss Mallard Mystery
By Robert Quackenbush

Dig to Disaster
Texas Trail to Calamity
Express Train to Trouble
Stairway to Doom

Little Goddess Girls
By Joan Holub and Suzanne Williams

Book 1: *Athena & the Magic Land*
Book 2: *Persephone & the Giant Flowers*
Book 3: *Aphrodite & the Gold Apple*
Book 4: *Artemis & the Awesome Animals*

Mack Rhino, Private Eye

Book 1: *The Big Race Lace Case*
Book 2: *The Candy Caper Case*

FORT BUILDERS INC.

HAPPY TAILS LODGE

by Dee Romito

ALADDIN QUIX

New York London Toronto Sydney New Delhi

For Bonnie, Jack, Linda, and Fred.
What a wonderful family you've built. —D.R.

ALADDIN QUIX
Simon & Schuster Children's Publishing Division
1230 Avenue of the Americas, New York, New York 10020
First Aladdin hardcover edition August 2020
Text © 2020 by Dee Romito
Illustration © 2020 by Marta Kissi
Also available in an Aladdin paperback edition.
All rights reserved, including the right of reproduction in whole or in part in any form.
ALADDIN and the related marks and colophon are
trademarks of Simon & Schuster, Inc.
For information about special discounts for bulk purchases, please contact
Simon & Schuster Special Sales at 1-866-506-1949 or business@simonandschuster.com.
The Simon & Schuster Speakers Bureau can bring authors to your live event. For
more information or to book an event contact the Simon & Schuster Speakers Bureau
at 1-866-248-3049 or visit our website at www.simonspeakers.com.
Jacket designed by Karin Paprocki
Interior designed by Mike Rosamilia
The illustrations for this book were rendered digitally.
The text of this book was set in Archer Medium.
Manufactured in the United States of America 0720 LAK
2 4 6 8 10 9 7 5 3 1
Library of Congress Control Number 2020938379
ISBN 978-1-5344-5242-8 (hc)
ISBN 978-1-5344-5241-1 (pbk)
ISBN 978-1-5344-5243-5 (ebook)

Cast of Characters

Jax Crawford: Part of the Fort Builders team

Amber & Dove Crawford: Jax's twin sisters

Mr. & Mrs. Crawford: Jax's parents

Caleb Rivers: Jax's best friend

Kiara Pal: Part of the Fort Builders team

Eddie Bell: Part of the Fort Builders team

Miss Pordum: Librarian at local library

Mrs. Rivers: Caleb's mom

Mrs. Newton: Runs Furry Friends pet rescue

Miss Berger: Owner of Veggie Bergers

Heidi: Owner of the bookstore

Contents

Chapter 1: A Big Surprise   1

Chapter 2: The Plan   12

Chapter 3: Testing It Out   28

Chapter 4: Problem-Solving   41

Chapter 5: All the Orders!   53

Chapter 6: What a Team!   64

Word List   84

Questions   86

STEM Activity   87

1

A Big Surprise

Jax Crawford could only stand the noise for so long.

His twin sisters were even louder than usual.

He went to see what they were so excited about.

"What's going on?" he asked.

"Mommy said we can get a pet!" said **Amber**.

"Really?" Jax loved the idea.

"And Daddy said we could get a pet too!" said **Dove**.

"So that's two pets!" added Amber.

Jax laughed. "You know it doesn't work that way, right? That still only means one pet."

The girls didn't pay any attention to him. They ran through

the kitchen screaming about the *two* pets they were getting.

Jax followed them into the backyard.

"Are we really getting a pet?" he asked his parents.

"Yes, we are," said **Mrs. Crawford** with a smile. "We decided you're all old enough to help take care of one."

"The girls want a kitten," said **Mr. Crawford**. "What do you think?"

Jax pictured running around the backyard with a dog. But a kitten would be great too.

"Kittens are cute," he said. "That'll be fun."

"Your sisters are very excited to name it," said his mom. "I hope that's okay."

"Sure," said Jax. Although he was a little disappointed that they didn't ask him. They'd never had a pet before. It was kind of a big deal.

"Can I go to Caleb's?" he asked.

"Of course. Say hello to his mom for me," said Mrs. Crawford.

Caleb Rivers was Jax's best friend. He lived just two houses away. It didn't take long to get there.

Caleb was sitting on the steps in his garage, tying his sneaker.

"Hey, Jax. I was heading to your house."

"I have news," said Jax. "We're getting a kitten."

Caleb had a houseful of animals. Two dogs, three cats, a bunny, a hamster, and five fish.

Although the number of fish was always changing.

"Kittens are the best," said Caleb. "But they'll get into all kinds of stuff."

"Like my sisters?" asked Jax.

The twins were always causing some kind of trouble.

"If your sisters climb up the curtains, knock things over, and chase each other around the house," said Caleb.

Both boys laughed.

"Yeah, I guess like your sisters,

then," Caleb confirmed.

Just then, their friends **Kiara Pal** and **Eddie Bell** rode up the driveway on their bikes.

A few weeks ago, they had all started a fort building company together: Fort Builders Inc. Whenever Kiara was visiting her grandmother down the street, they had an official meeting.

"What are you guys talking about?" asked Kiara.

"We're getting a kitten," said Jax.

"Oooh!" Kiara exclaimed. "I love cats!"

"I have a really good kitten treat recipe," added Eddie. "I can bake you some."

Everything Eddie baked was delicious. Probably even cat treats! **"That would be great,"** said Jax.

"Are you excited?" asked Kiara.

"Of course. I just feel a little left out," said Jax. "The girls get to name it, and I'm sure it'll sleep in their room. I'll probably get stuck changing the litter box."

"You could be in charge of brushing it," said Caleb. "Especially if you get a long-haired cat."

"You can pick out the toys," said Eddie.

They were great ideas. But they weren't *big* ideas.

"Thanks, but I'll think of something," said Jax. **"Let's start the meeting."**

Jax knew he'd figure it out. There's always a **solution** if you look hard enough. But it was time to focus on Fort Builders.

Kiara and Eddie got off their bikes and hooked their helmets onto the handlebars.

Caleb stood up. "The Fort Builders Inc., team is all here. I call this meeting to order."

2

The Plan

Their first job had been a box fort castle for a birthday party. The team had built three more forts since then. Which meant every-one had almost enough money to get what they'd been saving for.

But they also wanted more of a challenge.

"Maybe we can make something different," said Caleb. "Something that's not your usual fort."

Eddie leaned against a stack of boxes. Word about Fort Builders had spread quickly after their friend's party. Neighbors started dropping off boxes whenever they had them.

Kiara walked back and forth from one side of the garage to

the other. **"You're getting a kitten?"** she asked Jax.

Jax's eyebrows arched down. "Yeah."

"You're getting a kitten," she said as a **statement** instead of a question.

"I'm getting a kitten," Jax repeated. "Kiara, are you okay?"

Kiara stopped pacing. "And you want to do something to be part of it," Kira said.

Jax nodded slowly.

"It'll need a place to sleep," she said. "And play."

Eddie and Caleb looked confused too.

"Like a *pet fort*?" said Kiara.

"Like a pet fort!" yelled Jax. "Kiara that's brilliant!"

"We could totally build a pet fort," said Eddie. "What do you think, Caleb? You have a gazillion pets."

Caleb laughed. "My animals would love that," he said. "Well, maybe not the fish."

Kiara got out her sketch pad.

"Okay, so what are we thinking? What would a pet fort look like?"

"Maybe like a cat climber?" Caleb said. "Those tall things covered in carpet?"

They turned to Jax, their master builder.

"We'd have to keep it simple," he said. "And make sure it isn't too expensive."

"My rabbit loves hiding inside things," said Eddie. "I think we could use boxes."

Caleb got up and dug around

on a shelf. He pulled out a carpet square.

"What about these?" he said. "You peel the paper off the back and stick it. It's super easy!"

They passed around the carpet square.

"**I have so many ideas now!**" said Kiara. She sat down and sketched.

"**Me too!**" said Jax. He went over to the stack of boxes and searched through them.

"I could paint such fun things!" said Eddie.

Caleb loved seeing all of them excited about their new project. He was too!

Jax pulled a couple boxes from the pile. "Hey, Caleb. We might need to do some research."

Caleb opened the door and shouted inside. "Hey, Mom? Can you give us a ride to the library?"

The librarian at their local library helped the Fort Builders team find what they needed. **"This will get you started,"** said **Miss Pordum.** She set a stack of books and magazines on the table.

Caleb sorted them one at a time by topic.

"Here are a few websites that should help." Miss Pordum handed Jax a list.

"Thanks!" said Jax. He was excited to get started.

While Caleb and Eddie searched through the books, Kiara read pet blogs.

Jax watched step-by-step tutorials online.

. . .

By the time they got back to Caleb's house, they had a ton of ideas.

Kiara finished her sketch, and they made a plan.

They got the boxes they'd need.

They gathered up some carpet squares.

They carefully drew lines where the boxes had to be cut. But they needed a little help from an adult.

"You want me to cut along here?" asked Caleb's mom. She had her tools ready.

"Oh, yes, please!" said Kiara. **"Here's our plan."** She showed her the sketches.

As **Mrs. Rivers** did the cutting, the kids got the rest of their supplies together.

Jax supervised.

Mrs. Rivers moved on to the pieces for the ladder. Eddie heated up the hot glue gun.

Once they had the parts, Kiara and Eddie added each rung of the ladder. They stuck it together with the hot glue.

Caleb taped boxes together.

Jax added the curved pieces.

But of course, they couldn't have work time without the twins bursting in!

"What are you guys doing?" asked Dove.

"Can we help?" asked Amber.

After five years, Jax had gotten pretty good at telling them apart. But they were as identical as twins get. It helped that Amber usually wore her hair back and Dove wore hers down. Plus, Amber always wore something amber (a yellowish orange) and Dove wore white.

But sometimes they switched it up on purpose. They thought it was super funny. Jax thought it was super annoying.

"Dove, you can hold the sides of the ladder while Kiara and Eddie glue the steps on." Jax handed her two pieces. **"And Amber, you can help Caleb with the tape."**

The girls giggled.

"Okay, *Dove*. Go hold the sides of the ladder."

"Yeah, *Amber*. Go help with the tape."

Jax checked their hair. He checked their sock colors. But something was off.

He studied their faces. Their freckles. Their eyelashes.

"Let me see your toes," said Jax. The one thing Jax could always count on was the birthmark on Amber's big toe.

He looked right at the twin he was sure was Amber. **"Go help with the tape, Amber."** He turned to Dove. "Go help with the ladder, Dove." He didn't really care who did what, but he wasn't about to let them pull one over on him.

3

Testing It Out

The twins left long before the fort was finished. Once they saw how much work there was to do, they took off to play.

Which meant they had no idea the fort was really for the new kitten.

"The pet fort looks great!" said Caleb.

"Yeah, the kitten is going to love it," said Eddie. "Now we just need a name."

"For the kitten?" asked Jax.

"No, for the fort," said Eddie. "Something fun I can put on a sign for the front."

The four of them thought for a minute.

"I've got it!" shouted Kiara. "How about Happy Tails Lodge?

Get it? Instead of happy *trails*, it's happy *tails*."

Jax loved that idea. **"Happy Tails Lodge it is,"** he said with a big smile.

Caleb stood up. "We should test

the fort. We can do it here," he said.

"We could, but . . . give me a second," said Jax.

He ran home and was back a few minutes later.

"Well?" asked Kiara. "What's your idea?"

"I spoke to **Mrs. Newton**," said Jax. "She said we could try it out there!"

Kiara wasn't in the neighborhood enough to know what Jax was talking about.

"That's perfect!" said Eddie. He gave Jax a fist bump.

"Great idea!" said Caleb. He gave Eddie a high five.

The boys celebrated as Kiara tried to figure out what was going on.

"Hold on a minute." She put a hand on her hip. "Who is Mrs. Newton and where is 'there'?"

The boys laughed.

"Sorry," said Jax. "I forgot you don't know her. She runs the Furry Friends **pet rescue**."

"Ah. That makes sense," said Kiara. "I'm guessing there are kittens there?"

Jax nodded. "Yes. Lots of kittens. And no little sisters! My mom said she'd drive us over."

They put the kitten fort in

Mrs. Crawford's trunk and piled into the car.

"Hello!" shouted Mrs. Newton from the doorway. A big blue FURRY FRIENDS sign welcomed them from above a green awning.

"Thanks for letting us try out our pet fort," said Jax. **"Our friend Kiara designed it."**

"Wow. Nice to meet you, Kiara," said Mrs. Newton. "Let's bring your fort to the cat area."

The team carried the fort into a medium-size room in the back. There were kittens and older cats in roomy cages along the walls.

"The fort is a little small for the bigger cats," said Caleb. "But the kittens can use it for sure."

Mrs. Newton let out three of the kittens. Two black ones and an orange tabby.

They went for the fort right away. One of the black kittens hopped on top. The other two sniffed around the doorway.

Within a few minutes they were playing and even climbing up the ladder.

"I think they like it," said Jax's mom. **"Great job, kids."**

The team sat on the floor with

the kittens. The adults talked outside the glass door.

"Your new kitten is going to love it," said Eddie.

But before they could stop the

orange cat, it peed on the side!

"Um, Mrs. Newton?" Jax tried to get her attention by waving his hand and pointing.

She quickly opened the door and dashed inside.

"I'm so sorry," she said, picking up the kitten and putting it in a litter box. She gave the kitten a reminder. "Sometimes they smell something they don't like and mark their territory."

They couldn't give Jax's kitten

a fort that had been "marked" by another cat!

"It's okay," said Jax. "That was the point of testing it out."

"But the design was good," said Eddie. "They liked it."

"We'll just have to rebuild it," said Caleb.

"We have boxes in the back," said Mrs. Newton. "You can build it here if you'd like."

The group huddled up and whispered a few things back and forth.

"We'd like to take you up on that offer," said Kiara.

A **volunteer** carried the boxes outside for them. It was a beautiful day, and the awning was the perfect cover from the sun.

"Back to work, team," said Jax.

And back to work they went.

4

Problem-Solving

The team built the same pet fort they had before. But this time, they wanted the big cats to be able to play on it too.

They added some tunnels.

They added another ladder.

They added a scratching post.

"We should give it some fun details," said Kiara.

So they picked out cat toys to put inside the fort.

Eddie drew wood grain on the cardboard to make it look like real wood.

And Mrs. Newton gave them a soft round cushion to put on top.

It was amazing!

"You know, this doesn't have to be only for cats," said Caleb.

Just then, a little girl and her

dad walked up to their fort.

"This is so cool!" said the girl. "Bunny Foo Foo would love it!"

"Is it for sale?" asked the dad.

"Hold on a sec," said Jax. He turned to his friends.

They huddled together again.

"Should we sell it?" asked Jax.

"But it's for your kitten," said Caleb.

"I know, but we can build another one," said Jax.

"We've been wanting to grow

the business," said Kiara.

"We're getting pretty good at these," said Eddie. "It would be fun to make more."

With four thumbs up, they all agreed. **"Yes, it's for sale,"** said Jax to the dad. "Twenty dollars."

The girl jumped up and down while her father handed Jax a twenty-dollar bill.

"Great deal," said the dad. "You kids do nice work."

They helped him get it to his trunk, but there was a problem.

It was so big that it didn't fit!

They pushed and they pulled. They turned and they flipped.

"I'm really sorry," said the dad. **"We can't get this home."**

Everyone was disappointed. Plus, if he couldn't get it home, how could they?

The group gathered inside the cat room for a meeting.

"We need a plan B," said Kiara.

"What's a plan B?" asked Eddie.

"It's a backup plan," she answered. "When plan A doesn't work, you go to plan B."

"What if plan B doesn't work?" asked Jax.

"Then we'll need a plan C," answered Caleb.

All around them, the cats were sound asleep. Jax studied their cages.

"Our problem is that if it's too small, bigger animals can't use it," said Kiara.

"But if it's too big, no one can take it home," added Eddie.

Jax walked around the room quietly. He didn't want to wake the kittens.

They each had food, water, a bed, and a litter box. There was a shelf to jump on and toys to play with.

They were like little apartments. Some were separate, but

others were connected to one
another.

A fluffy white cat woke up and
walked through a hole to the next
cage.

Jax checked the sign on the
front for the cat's name. He leaned
in and whispered, **"You just
gave me an idea, Naboo."**
Jax turned toward his friends.
"We could build separate pieces.
But they'll connect together."

"That's brilliant," said
Kiara, keeping her voice down.

She took a sketch pad out of her bag. "Right. That way, they'll fit in a car or through a doorway," she added.

"And the customer can put it together however they want," said Jax.

Kiara sketched out a design.

"We can give them a suggestion on how to put them together," she said. "Or some people might like to design it on their own."

They all tiptoed out of the room.

"How'd the meeting go?" asked

Mrs. Crawford. "Are you about ready to go home?"

Jax shook his head. "Would it be okay if we did some more building at the store?"

"It's okay with me," said Mrs. Newton. "You've already attracted quite a crowd." She pointed outside where a big group of people were looking at their pet fort.

"We should get a sign out there!" said Eddie.

"There's poster board and

paint in the back room," said Mrs. Newton.

"We're on it!" The team raced to the back to get their supplies. Fort Builders was on to something big!

5

All the Orders!

Eddie's signs brought in even more people. Everyone loved the model pet fort.

The team even got some orders. Some interesting orders.

"I'd like a fort for my iguana,

please," said one customer.

"Can you make it a birdhouse?" asked another.

"Can you build me one for Shelly?" asked a little boy.

"Who's Shelly?" asked Jax.

"My turtle," answered the boy. "Shelly the turtle."

Jax giggled. "That's an awesome name," he said. "And yes, we can make one for Shelly."

Mrs. Crawford tapped Jax on the shoulder.

"Mom, I'm taking orders," Jax whispered. He went back to his customer.

His mom tapped him again. **"I need to tell you something."**

"Can I just finish this one?" he asked.

Mrs. Crawford nodded. She joined the volunteer who had come out to help cut boxes.

But Jax should have listened to what his mom had to say. Because they had a slight problem.

Two problems to be exact.

"I love it!" yelled Amber.

"I love it too!" shouted Dove.

Jax walked over to his dad. **"What are they doing here?"** he asked.

"I have to go to work," said Mr. Crawford. "Your mom asked me to drop off the girls. We didn't think you'd be here this long."

Jax could only imagine what kind of trouble the girls would stir up.

"I don't think this is a good idea," he told his dad.

"Sorry, bud. Maybe find something for them to do?"

Jax ran over to Caleb, Eddie, and Kiara.

"We have to keep my sisters busy," he said. **"Or they'll destroy the fort."**

They were already trying to crawl through one of the holes!

"I have an idea," said Kiara. "You finish the orders. I'll take care of your sisters."

Kiara walked over to the girls and handed them each a sheet of paper. She took colored pencils out of her bag.

They sat and drew. Quietly.

"How'd you get them to do that?" asked Jax.

"I told them they could earn a dollar each," she said. "If they design our best-selling piece."

It was a great idea. And totally worth it if it kept them out of trouble.

An hour later, the team had

eight orders! They'd given everyone a two-week time frame.

Using Kiara's designs, they got right to building.

They measured each box to make sure everything would fit together.

The more they worked, the more interest they had outside.

"I've never had such a busy day," said Mrs. Newton, poking her head out the door. **"Whatever you're doing, keep it up!"**

There were three more orders.

Then two more.

"We can't keep up," said Caleb. "We'll spend our whole summer building forts!"

"He's right," said Eddie.

"And I'm only at Nani's a few days a week," said Kiara.

Jax **scanned** through the orders. "Eddie, you'd better put 'Sold Out' on the sign."

"No problem," said Eddie.

In no time at all, the sign showed that they were closed for business.

Mrs. Crawford came outside with the twins. "How about a break for lunch at Veggie Bergers?" she asked.

Their neighbor **Miss Berger** owned the restaurant right next door. Everything on the menu was great, so it was an instant yes from the group.

They picked a window seat so they could keep an eye on things outside.

Soon, the table was full of food.

They talked about all the forts they'd be making.

They tried to figure out how to build one for a turtle.

They added up the money they'd make.

But the team was so busy

chatting that they had stopped watching the fort.

"Um, you guys . . ." Eddie pointed out the window. **"The Happy Tails Lodge is gone!"**

6

What a Team!

They rushed outside.

"Where did it go?!" Jax threw his hands in the air.

Everything else was still there. The boxes, the fort pieces, the sales table. Everything but the fort.

"Maybe Mrs. Newton brought it inside," said Caleb. "I'll go check."

Caleb ran inside while the others looked for the fort. But it was a sidewalk outside a shopping center. There was nowhere for it to hide.

"It's not inside," said Caleb, running out, breathless.

"Where could it be?" asked Eddie. "Do you think somebody took it?"

Kiara was over by the table, which had only a single dollar bill on top. **"Hmm,"** she said as she held it up.

She walked over to the **"Sold Out"** sign, which was facing the wrong way. When she turned it around, there was a big $1 written on it in red.

The twins **immediately** hid behind their mom.

"What did you do?" asked Jax. "Amber. Dove. What did you do?" he asked again.

"We just wanted to help you sell it," said Amber.

"Isn't that a good price?" asked Dove.

Jax couldn't believe it. The fort they worked so hard on—the fort for his new kitten—was gone. And all they had to show for it was one dollar.

The twins said they were sorry, but the fort was still gone.

Jax kicked at a piece of cardboard on the ground.

"We can build another one," said Eddie.

Mrs. Crawford put a hand on Jax's shoulder. "I'm really sorry. But I have to get the girls home soon."

Jax kicked at some cookie crumbs next to the cardboard.

"Why are there . . . ?" His words trailed off as he noticed more and more cookie crumbs. It was almost like a trail had been left. **"Where are you going?"** asked Kiara.

"Follow me," answered Jax.

They all followed behind him like a line of ducks.

The crumbs led the way to the bookstore down the sidewalk.

As Jax opened the door to the bookstore, the bell rang.

"Hello. Can I help you?" asked the woman behind the counter. Her name tag said HEIDI.

"We're looking for a missing pet fort," said Jax. "We followed a trail of cookie crumbs here."

"I think I might know where that came from." Heidi walked to the back of the store. She came out a minute later with a boy who looked just like her.

"Did you get that pet fort from these kids?" she asked him.

The boy shook his head. "No, Mom. I bought it from the Furry Friends rescue. For one dollar!"

Jax turned to the twins.

"Yeah, that was a mistake," he told the boy. "My sisters were playing with the sign."

"It's actually for their new kitten," added Caleb.

"It is?" said Amber.

"We didn't know *that*," said Dove.

Heidi told her son to go get the fort. "I apologize," she said. "He must have brought it in the back when I wasn't looking. He just got a new puppy."

The boy brought the fort out, as a little puppy followed. Its floppy ears swayed back and forth.

"You kids made this?" asked Heidi. "It's incredible."

"We did," answered Kiara.

"It's our business. Fort Builders Inc.," added Caleb.

"You know, I would love a fort for the store," said Heidi. "Maybe something that kids could read in?" **"We could totally do that,"** said Eddie.

The store was already amazing. It had a large kids' section, it was colorful, and the walls had huge **murals** of fairy-tale characters.

The little puppy weaved in and out of the fort doorways.

"If you want," said Jax, "we could sell you this fort too. We made it so big it won't fit in our car." Jax didn't want to sell the fort, but what choice did he have? **"I couldn't do that,"** said Heidi. "This is your fort. I can help you get it home. It'll fit in my van."

The smile on Jax's face stretched wide. His sisters gave each other an enormous hug as they jumped up and down.

"We'd really appreciate that," said Mrs. Crawford.

While the crew scouted out the bookstore for the best place for a fort, the adults put the Happy Tails Lodge in Heidi's van.

The team cleaned up what was left outside the pet rescue.

"I know we were going to wait to pick out the kitten," said Mrs.

Crawford. "But those little ones in there are so adorable. And it's an animal rescue organization, so we'd be doing a good thing."

Amber grabbed Dove's hand and pulled her aside. They whispered back and forth.

The two of them walked over to Jax.

"We want you to pick out the kitten," said Amber.

"Really?" asked Jax. "But you're so excited to choose one."

The girls smiled. "You made

such a nice fort," said Dove. **"We think you should do it."**

His sisters were annoying at times, but they had kind hearts.

Jax gave them a big hug.

The rest of the crew waited while Jax and his family went into the **feline** room.

They played with a bunch of kittens. But Jax kept going back to two little ones who were snuggling together in a cat bed.

The gray kitten had a little white spot under his neck. He

rubbed his head against the cage when Jax came close. The white one had brownish-orange spots and looked right at him.

"I can't decide," said Jax. "These two remind me of Amber and Dove. They're best friends. I don't want to separate them."

Jax put his finger up to the cage, and the white one put her paw out. She had an extra toe that looked like the thumb of a mitten. **"She's holding your hand!"** said Amber.

"She's a **polydactyl** cat," said Mrs. Newton. "It means 'many toes.'"

Just then, the gray kitten waltzed over and rubbed against Jax's hand.

"Mom," he pleaded. "What do I do?"

Mrs. Crawford asked if they

could take the kittens out.

Once they did, it was clear that those two kittens went together. Always together.

"We'll take them both," said Mrs. Crawford.

Amber and Dove leaped at Jax and wrapped their arms around him.

"Hey, what about me?" asked Mrs. Crawford. They all went in for a big family hug. "You'll have to help me explain this to your dad, though." She laughed.

The rest of the group piled into the room.

"We're getting two kittens!" yelled Amber.

The girls were right about getting two pets after all.

"What should we call them?" Jax asked the girls. "You can each name one."

The twins locked eyes. It was like they could talk to each other without words.

"We've decided," said Amber.

"The white one is Kitti, with an *i*," said Amber.

"And the gray one is Mo, with an *o*," said Dove.

Jax didn't really care what names they picked. He was just happy they all got to be a part of it. But he did love their choices.

"Kitti and Mo it is," said Mrs. Crawford.

"Let's get them home to the Happy Tails Lodge," said Jax.

Mrs. Crawford filled out all the paperwork and paid to cover the adoption fees. Jax picked out a few toys and some food to get them started. And without causing one bit of trouble, the girls carried the cat carrier to the car.

Kitti and Mo would be the official pet fort testers for Fort Builders Inc.

Jax leaned down to the carrier. **"Welcome to the team, little ones,"** he said.

He gave Mo a high five and Kitti a high six.

Word List

feline (FEE•line): Related to cats

immediately (ih•MEE•dee•uht•lee): Instantly

murals (MYUR•allz): Large paintings or other artwork usually created on walls

pet rescue (PET RES•kue): An organization that takes in stray animals and attempts to find them good homes

polydactyl (pah•lee•DACK•tuhl): Having more fingers or toes than normal

scanned (SKAND): Examined quickly

solution (suh•LOO•shun): The answer to a problem

statement (STAYT•mihnt): A stated fact or opinion rather than a question

volunteer (VOL•un•teer): Someone who helps willingly without asking to be paid

Questions

1. Why did Jax feel left out? What did he do to change that?

2. The team ran into a problem when their pet fort wouldn't fit in a car. What plan did they come up with to solve the problem for future forts?

3. There are several times when characters had to compromise or adjust their plans to reach an agreement. Which characters did this and why?

STEM Activity

How to measure a box:

Step 1: Gather a ruler or measuring tape.

Step 2: Position the box so the opening is on the top.

Step 3: Measure the side that is the longest from side to side. This is the length.

Step 4: Measure the side that is the shortest from side to side. This is the width.

Step 5: Measure the side that

runs up and down. This is the height.

Step 6: Put the measurements in this order: length times width times height. These are the dimensions of your box!

Bonus step: Multiply all three numbers and you'll get what's called the volume. Volume is the amount of space inside an object.